P9-DFS-043

THIS ONE 'N THAT ONE

in

Boing!

No Bouncing on the Bed

JANE SEYMOUR and JAMES KEACH

illustrated by
GEOFFREY PLANER

G. P. Putnam's Sons New York

G. P. Putnam's Sons, a division of Penguin Putnam Books for Young Readers,
345 Hudson Street, New York, NY 10014.
G. P. Putnam's Sons, Reg. U. S. Pat. & Tm. Off.
Published simultaneously in Canada.
Printed in the United States of America.
Designed by Marikka Tamura. Text set in Gill Sans.

Library of Congress Cataloging-in-publication Data
Seymour, Jane. Boing! No bouncing on the bed /
Jane Seymour and James Keach; illustrated by Geoffrey Planer.
p. cm.—(This one 'n that one)
Summary: Two naughty kittens bother their parents by jumping up and
down on all the beds and chairs in the house.
[1. Cats—Fiction. 2. Jumping—Fiction. 3. Behavior—Fiction.]
I. Keach, James. II. Planer, Geoffrey, ill. III. Title. IV. Series.
PZ7.S5235Bo 1999 [E]—dc21 98-55131 CIP AC
ISBN 0-399-23440-3
1 3 5 7 9 10 8 6 4 2
First Impression

To all our parents—
Mary and Stacy,
Lesley and George,
Oma Mieke, and of course Papa P!

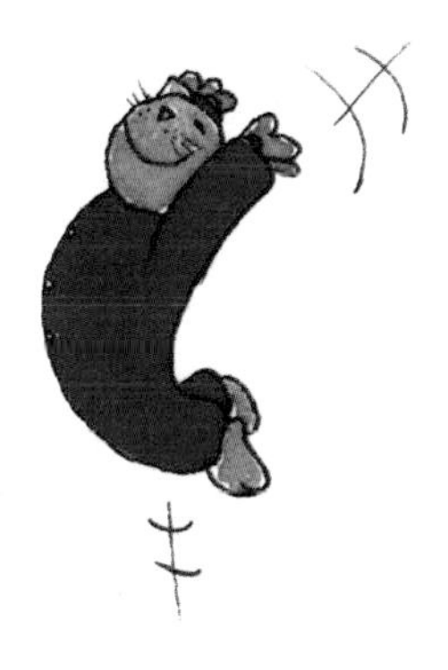

Boing!

THIS ONE jumped onto **THAT ONE**'s bed.

Boing!

THAT ONE jumped onto **THIS ONE**'s bed.

Boing!

THIS ONE bounced so high he could see the sea.

Boing!

THAT ONE bounced so high he could see a tree.

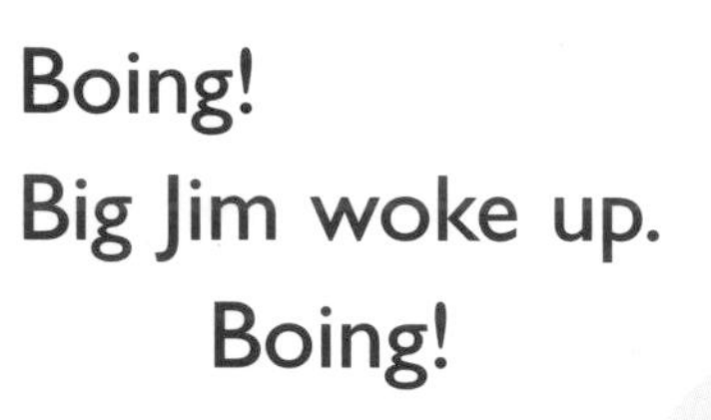

Boing!
Big Jim woke up.
Boing!
Lady Jane woke up.
"Jim, those naughty kittens are bouncing off the walls," she said.

“They’re just having fun,” yawned Big Jim,
and he went back to sleep.
Lady Jane tried to go back to sleep, but . . .

Boing!
Into the bedroom flew two dancing kittens!
Boing!
THIS ONE popped into Mom and Dad's bed.
Boing!
THAT ONE hopped onto Big Jim's head.
"Wake up Mom, wake up Dad," shouted
THIS ONE and **THAT ONE**.

"Hush you two—you'll wake the fish in the sea,"
said Lady Jane.
Big Jim tried to close his eyes again.
"Up!" said **THAT ONE**
as he pulled Dad out of bed.
"Hungry," said **THIS ONE**
as he pulled Mom out of bed.

So sleepy old Mom and sleepy old Dad rolled out of bed.

"C'mon Mom, c'mon Dad—jump with us," said **THIS ONE** and **THAT ONE** as they went downstairs for breakfast.

THIS ONE and **THAT ONE** managed to sit just a little bit still while they ate their food. When they bounced off it was Mom and Dad's turn. Big Jim cat was about to take a mouthful.

Boing!

Lady Jane was about to sip her tea.

Boing!

Big Jim thought that the noise sounded just like someone bouncing on his favorite chair.

BOING! BOING!

He put down his spoon and went into the living room.

It was not someone
bouncing on a chair.
It was TWO someones
bouncing on TWO chairs.

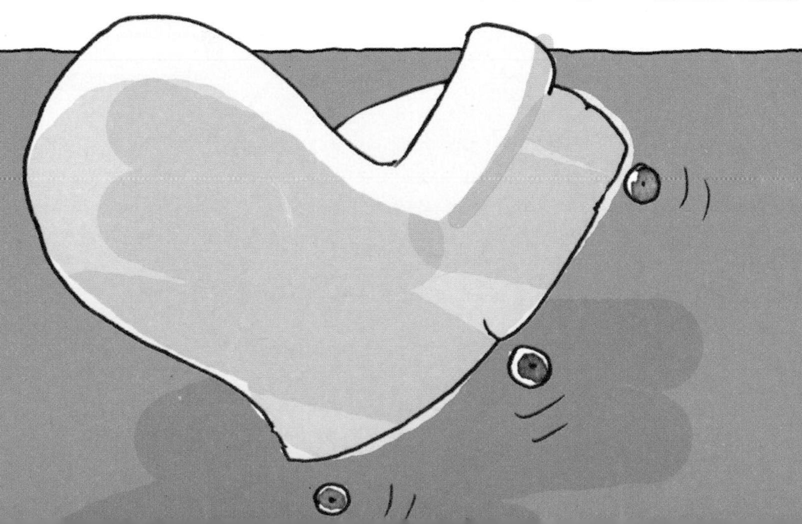

"Look at us, Dad!"
Wheeee! Boing! Wheeee! Boing!
"Hey, c'mon you two—no jumping on the chairs.
You'll break them," said Big Jim, and he turned
to go back to his breakfast.

Boing! Wheeee! Boing! Wheeee!
Big Jim looked around.
"Listen here kits, you stop this before Dad gets mad! I told you no bouncing on the chairs!" shouted Big Jim.

"But Dad, we're bouncing on the sofa,"
said **THIS ONE**.
Big Jim stared.
"OK, OK. No bouncing on the chairs
OR THE SOFA! Comprenez-vous?" he said.
THIS ONE nodded. **THAT ONE** nodded.

Big Jim Cat marched back to the kitchen.
He sat down, but before he could open his mouth,
he heard the noise again.
Boing! Wheeee! Boing! Wheeee!

He jumped from his seat and
leaped up the stairs two at a time.

There they were—
two naughty kittens jumping on a bed.
Boing! Wheeee! Boing! Wheeee!
"Listen you two. This is the last time I'm going to tell you. You may not bounce on the chairs or the sofa or your beds. OK?"

Big Jim stomped downstairs
and back to the kitchen.

“I don’t know how we got the naughtiest kits in Catafornia,” he said to Lady Jane.
“They’re just the bounciest kits in Catafornia,” she said.

Big Jim was about to sip his coffee when from upstairs came:
Boing! Boing! Boing! Boing!

"I do not believe it!"
he shouted.
"Don't get your whiskers in a twitch, dear," said Lady Jane.
"All right, all right. You stop them this time!" said Big Jim.
So Lady Jane went upstairs.

The noise stopped.
Big Jim smiled.
He opened up his copy of
Whiskers Weekly.
He took a sip of coffee.
He was about to eat his
breakfast when:
BOING! BOING!
BOING! BOING!

Big Jim
slammed down
the cup;
he leaped up
the stairs
three at a time.

He looked at **THIS ONE**'s bed;
He looked at **THAT ONE**'s bed—
but they weren't there.
BOING! BOING!
BOING! BOING!
The noise was coming
from *his* bedroom!

Big Jim ran to
the big bedroom
and flung open
the door!

There on the big bed was **THIS ONE** bouncing!
There on the big bed was **THAT ONE** bouncing!

And there in the middle was . . .

. . . Lady Jane bouncing!

BOING! Wheeeeeeeeeeeeeeeeeeeeeeeee!

"Oh, come on, Jim, have a Boing—it's good for your figure," said Lady Jane.
"Come on, Dad," said **THIS ONE** and **THAT ONE**.

"I guess if you can't beat 'em, join 'em," said Big Jim.

Big Jim took a little bounce.

Boing! It was fun!
Big Jim took a bigger bounce!

Boing! Boing! It was really fun!
Big Jim took a great big bounce!

CRACK!

Big Jim went right through the bed to the floor!

"Oh no!" said **THIS ONE**.

"Musn't bounce on the chairs," said **THAT ONE**.

". . . or on the sofa," said **THIS ONE**.

"...AND ESPECIALLY NOT ON THE BED,"
laughed Lady Jane.

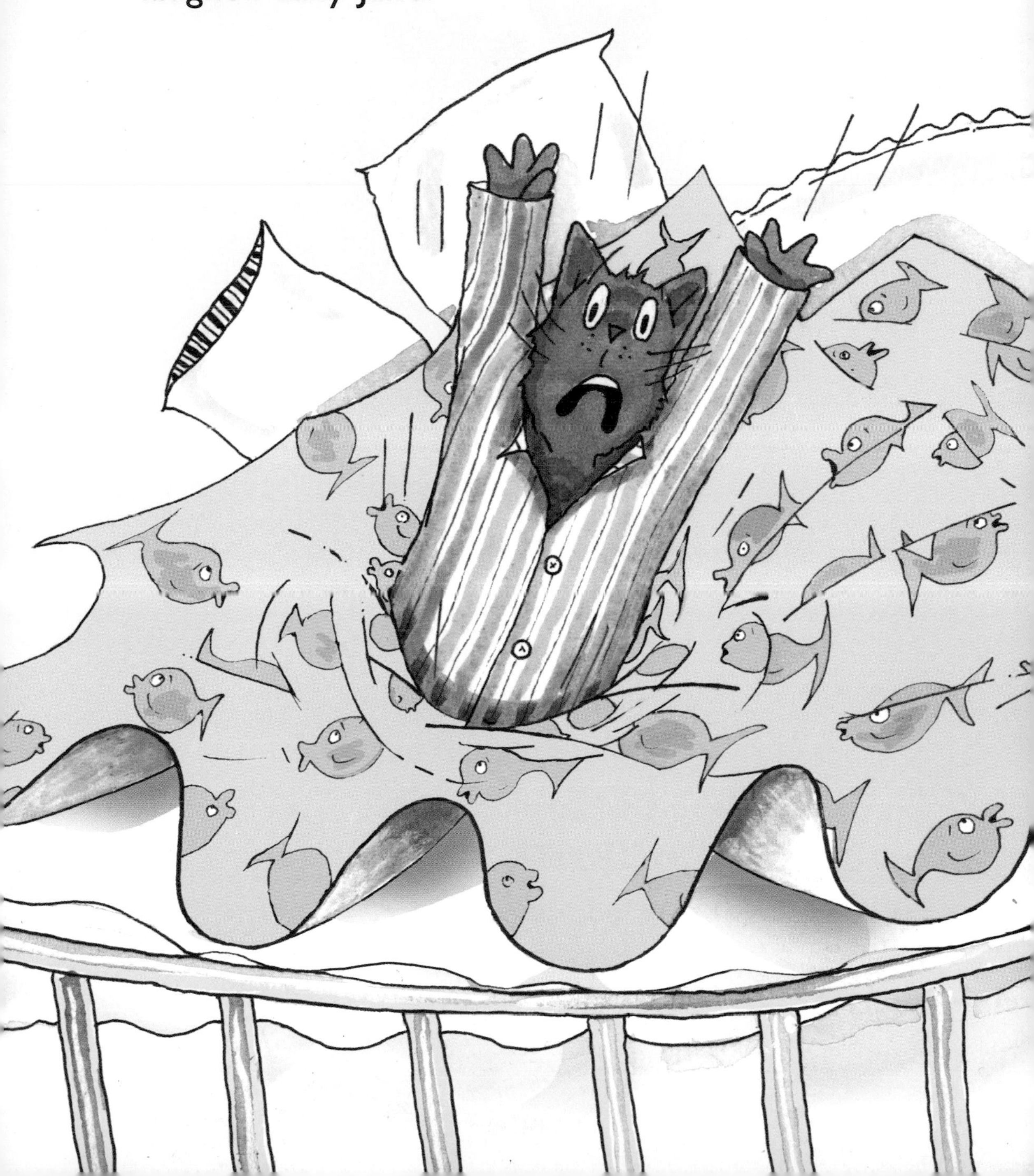

Bounce on the sofa,
Bounce on the chair.
THIS ONE *and* **THAT ONE**
Bounce everywhere.

Mom bounced too,
Dad bounced more.
BOIIIIIING! Oh no!
Dad's on the floor!